THE SILENT TREATMENT

It wasn't easy not speaking to her brother for two days, but Stevie was determined to keep up her silent treatment. He deserved it. The afternoon he had promised to come home for a practice session with Stevie he didn't show up until dinnertime. And the next day was Sunday, the day his own team had their practice. Stevie had gone to watch, planning to hang around the soccer field afterward with Dave and some of the other guys on the team. She thought for sure they'd get in some good practice with her then. But Dave had other plans.

"Gee, Stevie," he had said sincerely. "I'm sorry, but I promised Jill and Patty that I'd meet them at the movies. Wanna come along?"

"N-O spells no," Stevie said angrily.

P.S. We'll Miss You
Yours 'Til the Meatball Bounces
2 Sweet 2 B 4-Gotten
Remember Me, When This You See
Sealed With a Hug
Friends 'Til the Ocean Waves

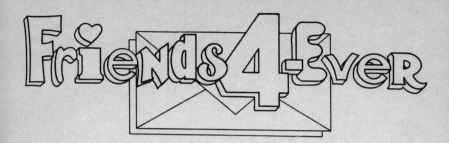

FRIENDS 'TIL THE OCEAN WAVES

Deirdre Corey

AN
APPLE
PAPERBACK

SCHOLASTIC INC.
New York Toronto London Auckland Sydney

ISBN 0-590-44028-4

12 11 10 9 8 7 6 5 4 3 2 1   0 1 2 3 4 5/9

Printed in the U.S.A   40

First Scholastic printing, December 1990

For Corey MacKenzie Aber
and
Kip Alexander Aber

EVERYTHING UPSIDE DOWN

Things had never looked so good to Stevie Ames. Standing on her head in the middle of her room, her long, reddish-blonde hair spreading around her, she saw everything in the room standing upside down. Her bed with the blue plaid spread, the beanbag chair in the corner, and her desk with the mess of old homework papers, pencil shavings, and soccer trophies all were undisturbed by the topsy-turvy position.

So far Stevie had been this way for 9 minutes 12 seconds. She was timing herself to see if she could break her own headstand record of 11 minutes 34 seconds. She knew she could do it if she just concentrated on something other than her shaking wrists and the itch on her left leg. Watching the timer bring her closer to her record, Stevie refused to let a silly old itch bring her down. "It doesn't itch. It doesn't itch. It doesn't itch," she said, squeezing her blue eyes shut, and trying not to think about the spot she wished didn't itch.

To take her mind off the feeling of pins and needles in her hands she opened her eyes and turned her head slightly so she could see her favorite poster on her wall. It was the one of a soccer player heading the ball. Stevie studied the way the player's head made contact with the ball right above the middle of his forehead. It was a perfect hit. Maybe if I can stand on my head just a little bit longer it will make my forehead stronger, she thought. Or more dented! She laughed to herself.

Standing on her head was only one of the things Stevie was better than good at. Soccer was another. In fact, Stevie was a soccer star at Crispin Landing Elementary School. Everyone said she was really good . . . for a girl. It was that "for a girl" part that really made Stevie mad.

She knew being a girl had nothing to do with being good or not being good at soccer. Her thirteen-year-old brother, Dave, was coaching her to help her prove that. In fact, all she had thought about for weeks now were the tryouts for the Select soccer team. If she could make the team, and she was sure she could, she would be the first girl to succeed. Both her brothers, Dave, and Mike who was eleven, had been spending all their time drilling Stevie in passing, kicking, heading, and stopping a soccer ball.

With only 1 minute 28 seconds to go to beat her headstand record, Stevie was feeling lucky to have two older brothers. As the timer ticked, Stevie thought about Dave. He was better than just a brother. He was a real friend, someone Stevie could talk to and always count on to be there for her when she needed him. Well, maybe not *always*. She needed him right now to cheer her through the last few seconds of this record-breaking contest. Stevie's wrists felt completely numb. Then the doorbell rang downstairs. Her mother's voice called up the stairs, "The girls are here!"

With only half a minute to go, Stevie did a somersault into an upright position and landed with a thud on her feet. All the blood that had rushed into her freckled face rushed back to where it belonged. Stevie shook her wrists and wiggled her fingers. She ran in place and shook her leg to get her jeans cuff back down over the spot that had itched. The itch was gone, but Stevie scratched it anyway as she ran down the stairs. The excitement of having her best friends, Molly Quindlen, Meg Milano, and Laura Ryder arrive a half hour earlier than they were supposed to made Stevie forget her record for the moment.

She bounded down the stairs calling out, "Friends 4-Ever, that's what we'll be!" She jumped down the last three steps and landed right in front of two older girls she had never seen before.

"Oh!" said Stevie to the two strangers. "I thought you were . . ."

"Friends forever?" One of the girls laughed.

Stevie felt a little embarrassed, but the feeling turned into immediate dislike for the girls. She couldn't believe anyone would want to walk around in public with their hair all sprayed and moussed up as these girls did. Looking closer, Stevie noticed some kind of purple gunk on their eyelids. She leaned right up into the face of the girl who had spoken. "There's something all over your eyes," she said. "Want a mirror to see it?"

The second girl spoke up. "She means your eye shadow."

Mrs. Ames interrupted what might have turned into an unpleasant exchange. "These are friends of Dave's," she explained firmly. She called up the stairs again, "Dave, the girls are here."

"Yeah," said Stevie, feeling a little confused. "For what? What did he do?"

The two girls started giggling. Stevie almost gagged right there in the hallway. Teenagers! she thought. Spare me from that terrible fate! Then she looked right into the face of the second girl and saw the same purple stuff. "Hey," she said. "That's funny. You've got the same problem!"

The girls' giggling was drowned out by the sound of Dave's feet clomping down the stairs. "Hey," he said, smiling. "How ya doing?"

"What happened to you?" gasped Stevie, looking at Dave's hair. She couldn't believe it. Dave, her own brother Dave, had his hair all sprayed and moussed up, too! And once she started noticing things, Stevie also noticed that Dave seemed to have on some kind of perfume! She couldn't even hold back the sneeze.

"You look great," Dave said to the girls, ignoring Stevie's question and her sneeze.

They do? thought Stevie, her eyes widening as she noticed her brother smiling in a different kind of way than she had ever seen him smile before. Doesn't he even notice all that gunk on their eyelids? she wondered in disbelief.

Dave seemed to realize that if he stayed one second longer, Stevie was going to say something horrible. He opened the door. "Ready to roll?" he asked, smiling that new smile again.

"Sure, Dave," said one girl sweetly.

"Yes, let's go. We want to get a good table at the library," said the other, leading the way out.

"See ya later, Mom," Dave said to his mother. He reached out a hand and ruffled Stevie's already messy hair affectionately. "See ya, Stevarino. Soccer practice this afternoon, right?"

"Right," Stevie answered glumly, smoothing down her rumpled hair. Stevie closed the door behind Dave and then leaned her back against it. Slowly she slid down the door into a squatting position on the floor. "Yeeecchh!" she said disgustedly. "Who were *they*?"

"Oh, Stevie." Her mother laughed. "They're darling girls. They're just Dave's friends from school. They called earlier to ask if he wanted to go with them to the library to study, that's all."

"Well, I hope they're studying beauty hints!" snapped Stevie. "I don't think a hurricane could move those hairdos of theirs!" Stevie couldn't hide her feelings. She was jealous. Ever since her parents were divorced, when Stevie was only two years old, Dave had always treated his little sister like she was special. He taught her soccer, basketball, football, bike riding, everything.

"What's he want to be hanging around with girls for, anyway?" she sputtered to her mother.

Before Mrs. Ames could answer, the front door opened, pushing Stevie out of the way. It was Stevie's other brother, Mike. "Wow!" he said. "Who were those two girls with Dave?" Bouncing the basketball he held in one hand, Mike gave a low whistle of approval before heading for the kitchen for a snack.

"Just friends," said Mrs. Ames.

"Nice friends!" Mike called from inside the refrigerator.

"If you like that kind of thing," Stevie said under her breath. She didn't want Mike to hear her say that, just in case he *did* like that kind of thing. I don't think I could take both of them cracking up at the same time, she thought. Having girls hanging around to be with her brothers was something new.

"*Really* nice friends," Mike added, dropping a piece of rolled-up ham into his mouth as he headed out the door again.

Mike's reaction was the last straw for Stevie. She turned and ran up the stairs to the safety of her room. She went over to the bedside table and picked up the framed photograph that stood next to the white shaded lamp. It was a picture of Dave. He was kneeling with a soccer ball on his knee and one arm resting across the ball. He wasn't smiling, although he should have been. This picture had been taken the day Dave's soccer team won the championship game. It had been Dave who scored the winning goal. He was wearing what he now called his "Winning Shirt." It was bright red with a big white number

12 on it. Stevie loved that shirt. Dave had promised that she could have it if she made the Select soccer team. She loved the shirt and she loved Dave, but that didn't stop her from turning the photo facedown on the table. Then she went over to the timer, set it for 11 minutes 35 seconds, put her head down on the floor, spread out her long hair, and lifted both legs up into the air.

"Things definitely look better upside down," she said out loud. "Even you do, David Ames," she said, sticking out her upside-down tongue at the picture.

Just as the pins and needles were starting to sting her flat-on-the-floor palms, Stevie heard the doorbell ring again. Once again, her mother's voice called up, "The girls are here."

"What girls?" Stevie asked, cautiously this time.

The answer came in the sound of three pairs of feet running up the stairs and three familiar giggles drifting through the hallway. Still standing on her head, Stevie looked toward the doorway and saw her three friends, Molly, Meg, and Laura, standing upside down and laughing.

"What do you mean 'what girls?' " demanded

Meg, straightening the barrette in her blonde curly hair. "Are there any other girls besides the fabulous Friends 4-Ever?"

Stevie smiled weakly as she flipped herself right side up again. For some reason, even standing upright, she felt as if her world had been turned a little upside down. Seeing her brother looking like he had had made Stevie's stomach feel a little strange. It wasn't just the way he looked that made her feel funny. It was the way he looked at the two *girls*. Seeing those girls looking back at him in the same way had made her stomach turn over completely. Stevie couldn't explain it even to herself, but the moment Dave smiled that smile her own refused to come out again.

Stevie glanced at the faces of her laughing friends. Then, catching a glimpse of her own not-so-happy face in the mirror, she couldn't help thinking, It's times like these when friends matter most.

4 FRIENDS' FEELINGS

Stevie was right. Her three best friends could see right away that Stevie was upset.

"What's the matter, Stevie?" Molly asked, being the first to stop giggling. "You look like you've seen a ghost or something." She pushed back her short, dark hair.

"Except you're not white, you're all red," added Meg.

"I'm red from standing on my head," Stevie explained unnecessarily. "And I haven't seen a ghost. I've seen something worse!"

"Worse?" wondered Laura aloud. "What did

you see? Two ghosts?" All the girls laughed except Stevie.

"Close," said Stevie. "Two teenage girls wearing fright wigs and swamp gunk on their eyelids."

"Where'd you see that?" Meg asked. "In the movies?"

"No, right here in my own house. And the even worse part is that they were here to see my brother Dave. And the even worse, worst part is he thought they looked good!" Stevie threw her hands up in disbelief.

"He did?" Molly said, also finding it hard to believe.

"And so did my mom," Stevie added. "She said they were 'darling.' Yeecchh!"

"She did?" Laura said, adding her own amazement.

"And, believe it or not, so did Mike!" Stevie added.

"He did?!" said Meg, Molly, and Laura together now.

"Why'd they have wigs on?" Meg asked.

"And swamp gunk?" Laura asked. "What is swamp gunk, anyway?"

"Okay, okay," Stevie said, laughing a little at

herself. "So maybe they weren't wearing wigs. But they both had their hair sprayed and full of styling mousse or gel or something that made it stand up straight. And the swamp gunk was eye shadow, but it was purple, which is what the wicked queen in *Snow White* wears. I thought they both looked *terrible*, but what do I know? Dave and everyone else liked them."

"They sound pretty bad to me," said Meg.

"Me, too," Laura agreed, pushing her long brown hair behind her shoulders.

"But you look better now, Stevie," Molly said. "Your face isn't so red anymore. And before you get red all over again from talking about those girls, whoever they are, how about a club meeting?"

"My favorite two words," Meg said. "I now call this Friends 4-Ever club meeting to order," Meg said in her usual takeover tone of voice.

"Good idea," muttered Stevie, flopping down on her blue rug. For as long as all the girls could remember they had always had clubs. One summer they had the Clue Club and spent their days looking for mysteries to solve. In the fall they started a Gypsy Club and collected fortunes from Chinese fortune cookies. When they felt like making crafts Meg formed a club to sell what they made.

All the clubs had been fun, but none had lasted as long as the club they now had, the Friends 4-Ever Club. It had all started when Molly announced she was moving to Kansas until her grandfather, who was sick, was well enough to take care of his hardware store again. Her family had thought it would only be for a few months, but those months stretched into many more. All that time the girls kept their friendship strong in letters they sent back and forth between Rhode Island and Kansas. Each of them now had stacks of letters. Stevie's were written on sneaker-decorated paper; Meg's were on kitten stationery. There were unicorn letters from Laura, and rainbow ones from Molly.

At last, after many letters, Molly had come back. The long letters stopped, but the girls never stopped sharing their feelings. It was Molly's great idea to write little notes to each other in what she called The Secret Note Society. She told Stevie, Laura, and Meg all about it in notes she left in special places. Meg found her first note in the knothole of a fence post in her yard. Laura's first note appeared one morning in the chimney of a birdhouse in her yard. And when Stevie climbed her favorite tree, she found a note Molly had left there for her:

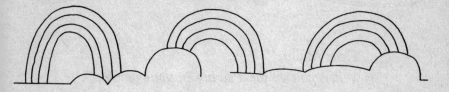

THE SECRET NOTE SOCIETY
Dear Stevie,
    Look for notes every day
    Hidden in the tree this way.
    I'll write to you in your tree,
    Now you find a spot to write to me!
                    Friends 'til the Fire Flies,

Molly

Stevie was thrilled when she found the note, and immediately jumped down from the tree and ran inside to get her stationery with the blue high-top sneakers on it. After thinking for a long time, she wrote back to Molly.

Dear Molly,
When you go for a swing in your hammock
*   next time*
Look for a special Stevie Ames rhyme.
I'll leave my notes in your favorite spot
Where the fringe of the hammock is tied in a
*   knot!*
*   Yours 'til the Dogwood Tree Barks,*

STEVIE

Laura and Meg quickly caught on to the idea of leaving secret notes for each other. Now, instead of checking their mailboxes every day as they did when Molly was away, each checked her own secret letter spot. They all knew each others' hiding places and left notes, letters, jokes, and other surprises often. The best things were shared at club meetings.

"I'll start, this time," said Meg, unfolding a

16

note written on Laura's unicorn stationery. "Obviously it's from Laura, and I think we can help her solve a problem at this meeting."

"That's what I was hoping you'd say," Laura said.

Meg began to read aloud.

Dear Meg,

In two weeks and one day I'll be having my birthday party. Now that Molly is finally home I want this year's party to be more special than ever. The problem is I can't decide what kind of party to have. Some kids go to bowling alleys or to the movies, but I definitely want to have my party at home. Got any ideas? I know I can count on you all to make this the best party ever, right?

Your Friend 4-Ever,

Laura

"Hey," said Molly, "I have a note from you that says the exact same thing, Laura."

"Me, too," Stevie said, as they each unfolded their own copy of Laura's note.

"Well, I figured if I wrote you all the same note you'd all think about the party and come up with some great ideas at this meeting," Laura explained. "So, did you all think?"

Meg jumped up. "I know! How about a Treasure Hunt Party?"

"Or a Backwards Party," Molly said, pushing her short hair back out of her eyes.

"Well, I think a great party would be a soccer party," Stevie said, giving her foot a kick forward. "I'd come to that."

"Oh, Stevie," Molly said, "you'll come to whatever kind of party Laura has. You know that."

"True," said Stevie, walking over to Dave's picture and turning it faceup again.

"How about a Ballet Party?" Laura said excitedly. "We could all wear leotards and ballet shoes and — "

"Tutus?" Stevie finished for her. "Wait just a minute. Me in a tutu? No way. But if you have

18

a Ballet Party, I'll come cheer for you all!"

"That's it!" Meg shouted, jumping up and down. "Laura, Stevie just had the best idea of all!"

"I did?" Stevie said, putting her finger to her temple questioningly.

"She did?" Molly wondered, too.

"Yes!" Meg bubbled. "Laura, you're going to have a cheerleading party! I just heard my mother talking about some of the cheerleaders from the junior high school who come to parties and teach cheerleading. Won't that be great to learn real cheers and all the jumps and everything?"

Now Molly and Laura joined in the excitement. "Perfect!" Laura agreed as she pranced across the room, crossing her arms and jumping with an arched back.

"You almost don't need lessons," Molly said admiringly. "But what a great idea. Stevie, you're a genius!"

Stevie lifted her eyebrows quizzically as she wondered, one, what the excitement was all about over cheerleading; and two, why she was getting all the credit for the idea just because she said the word *cheer*? She decided to accept the credit. "Glad to be of service," she joked, taking a deep bow.

In all the excitement, Stevie had almost forgotten how miserable she had been feeling before the girls had arrived. Now, as she bowed she stole a peek at her clock. It was close to one-thirty already!

"I'm starved," said Stevie, "and it's no wonder. We missed lunch."

Just then Mrs. Ames' voice called up. "Girls? What about some lunch? You've been locked up there in that room for hours. I've got sandwiches ready, so come on down."

Without any more encouragement, the four friends went tearing down the stairs, taking their party ideas with them. As they sat around the kitchen table talking excitedly about Laura's party, the front door opened and Dave came in out of breath.

"Mom? I already ate at Jill's house. We're all going over to Patty's to listen to some new tapes, okay?" Dave didn't even wait for an answer. He opened the refrigerator door, took a swig of orange juice straight from the container, and turned to hurry back out.

"But what about our soccer practice?" Stevie called after him, her words muffled by a mouthful of peanut butter-and-jelly sandwich.

"Later, Stevie," Dave yelled back. "Gotta run, they're waiting for me." The front door slammed, and Dave was gone. Meg and Laura began talking and laughing again. Molly, who understood Stevie better than anybody did, quietly watched her friend blink to hold back the stinging tears of disappointment. Molly reached out a hand and patted Stevie on the shoulder but said nothing.

Stevie looked up at Molly and saw her face through a blur of tears. "I guess I just want to be by myself now," she said softly.

"Okay, guys," Molly said briskly to the other two girls who were so wrapped up in their talk of cheers and jumps that they didn't notice Stevie's change in mood. "Let's head over to my house now. Stevie, if you want to come later just come on."

"I'll be practicing with my brother so I can't come later," Stevie said, pulling herself together so the others wouldn't see that she had cried over something so silly.

After clearing their dishes from the table, the

girls filed out of the house leaving Stevie behind.

"He'll be back in a while, Stevie," said her mother, brushing her daughter's hair back from her eyes.

"Yeah. Sure." Stevie sighed as she headed back up to her room. When she got there she reached into her desk drawer and pulled out a piece of her sneaker stationery. Without even thinking for a minute, Stevie wrote:

> Dear Molly,
>   Knock knock.
>   Who's there?
>   Sock.
>   Sock who?
>   Sock my big brother, that's who.
>   Yours 'til the Kitchen Sinks,
>
>   STEVIE

She folded up her note and glumly walked

downstairs. Grabbing her Red Sox sweatshirt and throwing it over her shoulder, Stevie quickly changed her mind and headed for Molly's house to join her friends. But first, she stopped at the hammock and stuffed her note into Molly's secret hiding place, the spot where the fringe was tied into a knot.

3

THE SILENT TREATMENT

It wasn't easy not speaking to her brother for two days, but Stevie was determined to keep up her silent treatment. He deserved it. The afternoon he had promised to come home for a practice session with Stevie he didn't show up until dinnertime. And the next day was Sunday, the day his own team had their practice. Stevie had gone to watch, planning to hang around the soccer field afterward with Dave and some of the other guys on the team. She thought for sure they'd get in some good practice with her then. But Dave had other plans.

"Gee, Stevie," he had said sincerely. "I'm sorry, but I promised Jill and Patty that I'd meet them at the movies. Wanna come along?"

"N-O spells no," Stevie said angrily.

"Aw, don't be mad, Stevie. I promise you I'll practice with you after school tomorrow. Just you and me, okay?"

"I already have plans. Sorry." And she had walked off in a huff.

That night at dinner she pretended she didn't even hear him when he described what the movie was about. He knew she was trying hard not to talk to him or even listen to him, so he couldn't help but tease her a little. After everything he said he added, "Right, Stevie?" or "What do you think, Stevie?"

No answer.

Dave tried the things that usually got a giggle out of Stevie. First he tried the old Hertz doughnut trick on her.

"Hey, Stevie," he said. "Want a Hertz doughnut?"

No answer.

Then he gave her a couple of friendly punches on the arm and said, "Hurts, don't it?" He laughed at his own joke, but he was laughing alone. Stevie sat stone-faced. Mike knew he shouldn't laugh and that if he did Stevie would probably jump on him. He tried to hold back his smile. But Dave wasn't finished with Stevie. Next he said, "Hey! Guess who's back?"

No answer.

Dave slapped Stevie on the back as he laughed and said, "*Your* back!"

Mike couldn't hold it in any longer. He exploded with laughter, which only made Stevie angrier. She ran up the stairs yelling, "You'll be sorry if I get to your rooms first!"

Both Dave and Mike shot up the stairs after her, hoping to stop her from doing whatever she was planning to do to their rooms. Dave caught her just as she was about to pull his favorite poster off his wall. Stevie slipped out of his grasp and ran into her own room, slamming the door behind her. From that second on she promised herself she'd never speak to him again, ever.

Now it was Tuesday night and he was doing everything he could to get back on her good side. Every time she opened her bedroom door she found some other peace offering outside. First there was his favorite soccer trophy. She took it and put it on her desk next to her own smaller trophies, but she still didn't talk to him. Next she found the leather batting glove she always borrowed from him. She took that, too, but still wouldn't talk. The pile on her desk grew to include Dave's best pen, his old Rubik's cube, the poster Stevie had almost ripped off the wall, and a candy bar. None of these things made her break her silence. What finally did it was a simple note. All it read was, *Dear Stevie, Will ya be my friend? Love, Dave.*

"David Ames!" Stevie yelled into the hallway.

Dave opened the door to his room slowly and poked his head out. He could see Stevie standing there, feet planted solidly on the floor and hands on her hips. He could also see that she had a big smile on her freckled face. Dave dared to come all the way out of his room, and Stevie stuck out her hand for a let's-make-up handshake. Now Dave's smile widened as he, too, stuck his hand out to shake with Stevie. Just as he was about to grasp her hand, Stevie stuck her thumb out and pulled her hand back over her shoulder out of Dave's reach. They both laughed with relief at finally having the long fight over with. Mike came out to see what the laughing was all about and made some remark about giving peas a chance instead of peace a chance. At last, things in the Ames' household were back to normal.

But it didn't last long.

Things went pretty smoothly for the next few days. Every day after school both Dave and Mike worked with Stevie on her ball control. It was important for her to practice moving the ball with her feet while looking down the field toward the goal.

"Keep your eyes ahead of you," Dave directed, as Stevie moved the ball along the grass in the front yard. "Don't let anything distract your attention from that goal. If you take your eyes away even for a second someone will have it."

Stevie concentrated and did exactly what Dave told her to do. Mike played against her, trying to steal the ball. He was only able to about half the time. Every day Stevie got better and better.

"You're gonna be in great shape for the Select preliminary tryouts tomorrow," Dave assured her.

"Do you really think so?" Stevie asked worriedly, hoping the answer would be yes.

"For sure," Dave said. "You're terrific, Stevie.

If you make it through the game tomorrow without getting cut from the list of finalists you'll have as good a chance as anyone. And just remember, if you need me, I'll be there watching."

Stevie went to bed that night feeling good. All the practice had tired her out enough so that she could sleep, even though excitement should have kept her awake.

When the alarm rang in the morning, Stevie was wide awake immediately. She rushed through morning teeth brushing, ran a comb through her hair, and put on her soccer uniform that her mother had laid out the night before. First she pulled on the white shorts with the black-and-white soccer ball on one side. Next she slipped into the royal-blue T-shirt with the number 3 on the back. Last she put on the shin guards, and high white socks with the royal-blue bands. She took a look at herself in the full-length mirror on the inside of her closet door.

"You look like a winner to me," Dave said, coming up behind her and adding his reflection to hers.

"Thanks," said Stevie, closing the door and thinking how funny it would be if the mirror image of herself and Dave were really stuck in the closet. She opened the door and checked the mirror just to see. Gone, except for her own face peeking around the door.

"Let's move it," Dave said, hurrying Stevie along.

"I'm coming. I'm all ready. I'm — " Stevie's excited replies were interrupted by the doorbell and then the rush and rumble of a lot of feet coming up the stairs.

"Are you ready?" Meg said, barging into Stevie's room with Molly and Laura piling up behind her. All three girls looked excited.

"This is *your* day, Stevie, and we're here to cheer for you!" Laura did a jump.

"We wanted to get there early, so we could get the best spots on the sidelines," Molly said. "We hope we bring you good luck."

"You might have to bring me *there*," Stevie laughed. "I'm sooo nervous!"

"Here," said Molly, handing Stevie a tiny horseshoe sticker. "I brought this from my Kansas 'N' Stuff box. Wear it on your shirt for good luck."

Mike came up behind the girls and stood in Stevie's doorway. "We'd better go now," he said. "This is going to be a big deal. Everybody is going to be there, especially since they're trying out all the Select teams today. It'll be packed at the field."

"Well, then," said Stevie, pushing through to get out, "then I say let's go, let's go, let's . . ."

"G-O!" shouted Molly, Meg, and Laura in unison with Stevie.

Dave and Mike both held their hands over their ears practically the whole way to the field because the four friends were shouting, "Let's go, Stevie, let's go!" in a chanting cheer that made Stevie feel like the winner Dave said she was.

STEVIE GETS HURT

The sounds of the girls' singing, laughing, and cheering reached the soccer field before they did. Stevie was the first to stop the noise when she saw the size of the crowd already at the field. Kids of all ages and sizes covered the field, creating a rainbow effect with all their different-colored uniform shirts.

"I told you it would be packed," Mike said as he and Dave caught up to the girls. "Stevie, just remember it's speed and ball control that count and you've got that."

"Just keep your eye on the ball and concentrate on moving it down the field," Dave coached. "You watch the ball, and I'll be watching *you*."

"And don't forget we love ya," Molly called out after Stevie, who was hurrying over to the tables where the soccer officials were checking in the players who were trying out. Standing in line Stevie got a good look at the competition. These players were all the best, the toughest, and the roughest. Stevie wasn't worried. She knew she was prepared. Just as she was above to give her name to the official behind the table, a much bigger girl bumped into Stevie, causing her to slam her wrist hard against the table's edge.

"Ouch!" cried Stevie, rubbing her wrist to make the stinging go away.

"Oh, sorry about that," the big girl grunted as she ran off to take her place on the field.

Molly, Meg, and Laura ran over to where Stevie stood. "We saw that!" Molly fumed. "What was she trying to do, squash you before the game?"

"Are you all right?" Laura asked, concerned as Laura always was about *everybody*, looking at Stevie's wrist.

"Yeah, I'm all right," said Stevie. "But she sure is big, isn't she?"

"She can't be in the same age group as you, can she?" Meg asked.

"That's what I'm about to find out," said Stevie, as it became her turn to register for the tryouts.

The man seated behind the table looked up, smiled at Stevie, and said, "Well, so *you're* the other girl trying out. Good for you and good luck to you."

Stevie gave the man her name, team name, and her age. Then she asked, "Is the other girl playing in the older group?"

"Nope," answered the man. "She'll be playing in your group but on the opposite team. Better hurry now, they're getting into position."

"Oh, Stevie," cried Molly, throwing her arms around her friend. "Good luck. I know you're gonna do great."

"We'll be cheering for you," Meg added.

"Just remember, we're on your side." Laura smiled her sweet smile.

"Then I can't lose," Stevie said confidently, as she sat on the grass and put on her cleats. "Thanks, guys."

Taking her position on the field, Stevie looked to the sidelines and saw Dave and Mike waving and giving her the thumbs-up sign. She returned the sign quickly and then gave her attention to the referee. In a minute the whistle blew and the ball was in play.

Stevie wasted no time. She darted forward and quickly caught the ball with the side of her foot. Dribbling down the field toward the goal, Stevie passed it to another player who was right in front of the goal. He slammed the ball directly through the goalie's legs into the goal. Stevie's great assist helped her team get the first goal. Her brothers and friends screamed from the sidelines as they jumped up and down. Stevie was doing all right out there, and they were proud of her.

Stevie's brothers and friends weren't the only ones to see her great play. The big girl on the other team figured out quickly that Stevie was the one to watch out for. For the rest of the first quarter and the second, the girl stuck to Stevie like glue, blocking her passes and standing way too close for Stevie's comfort. Despite the heavy guarding Stevie was still able to help keep the ball away from the other team. By halftime, Stevie was flushed and panting with excitement.

As she gulped down water and ate orange slices, Dave filled her ears with more helpful hints about scoring goals.

Molly and the other girls came running over to congratulate Stevie. "You were fabulous!" Molly shouted. "I knew you were good, but I didn't know you were *great*."

"Did you hear us cheering for you?" Laura asked.

"All I could hear was that big guard breathing down my neck," Stevie answered breathlessly.

"That girl is awful!" Meg sputtered. "She won't stay away from you!"

"Just watch out for her, Stevie," Molly warned. "It looks like she's out to get you."

"No," Dave said. "She's out to *stop* her. But you just keep up the good work, Stevie." Before anyone could say anything else, the whistle blew again signaling time for the third quarter to begin. Stevie exchanged high fives with Molly, Meg, Laura, Dave, and Mike and she ran back onto the field. Within seconds the big girl was right behind Stevie.

"Watch out, Stevie!" Meg yelled from the sidelines. "She's right behind you!"

Stevie didn't need Meg to tell her about the

girl. She could feel her around her no matter which way she turned. It didn't matter at that moment because the boys on the team had the ball in play. One boy kicked the ball downfield, and the big girl guarding Stevie broke away and went after it. With a quick kick of her foot she had the ball to herself and was taking it the other way. Ten more feet and it would be a goal. The big girl slowed down to get control of the ball as she lined it up for the shot into the goal.

Stevie saw her chance and took it. She darted ahead and easily stole the ball back. The crowd on the sidelines roared their approval of Stevie's great play. But the big girl wasn't about to let Stevie get away with the ball. She caught up and bumped against Stevie as hard as she could. Stevie looked to the sidelines for some help from Dave. What she saw startled Stevie. Instead of watching her, Dave was laughing and talking to the two girls who had come to the house the other day! In a flash Stevie realized that one of the girls was wearing Dave's Winning Shirt! The shirt he was supposed to give to her!

"Hey — " Stevie started to yell. But before she could get the rest of her angry sentence out, something heavy fell full-force against her. Afterward nobody was really sure if the big girl tripped Stevie on purpose or not. Her foot *did* go out, and Stevie *did* fall down. Tears stung her eyes as the girl followed her down to the ground and landed right on top of her ankle. A sharp pain shot through Stevie's foot as it twisted under the weight of the girl. The whistle blew for a time-out. Meg, Molly, and Laura hurried to Stevie's side.

"You tripped her!" Molly yelled at the big girl.

"Are you all right, Stevie?" Laura cried. "Can I help you?"

Stevie looked up and saw Dave running toward her. "What happened?" he shouted. "I didn't see what happened! Are you all right, Stevie?"

Stevie was determined not to let Dave see that her feelings were hurt almost as badly as her ankle. Quickly she wiped away her tears, saying, "I'm okay." She tried to stand with the help of her friends. "Ouch." She winced as she collapsed against Dave and Mike. Stevie heard the whistle blow when she was off the field.

The game was continuing without her.

"You were really terrific, Stevie," Dave said, trying to make up for missing her accident.

"How would *you* know?" Stevie grumbled back at him.

"We'd better get you home," Molly said. "You can lean on me."

"And me," added Meg.

"And me, too," Laura said.

"Thanks," said Stevie as tears started filling up her eyes again. There was no singing or laughing or cheering from the group on the way home. In silence, the four friends and Stevie's brothers made their way slowly back to Stevie's house. When at last Stevie was settled in a chair with her foot up, she watched her ankle swell and her chances of being in the final tryouts shrink.

FRIENDS IN NEED

From where she sat, propped up by a mountain of pillows in her bed, Stevie had a good view of all the special treatment her sprained ankle had gotten her so far. She saw the portable TV set up at the end of her bed. As far as she was concerned the TV was no good after nine A.M., anyway, because on school days there was nothing on except silly soap operas.

Next to her bed was a snack table with a breakfast tray holding a half-eaten blueberry muffin and an untouched glass of orange juice. A lunch tray sat next to the breakfast tray. Stevie had eaten all of the tuna fish sandwich except the crusts, but the pickle chips and apple slices stayed in their fanned arrangement on the plate.

On a stool by her night table there was a pile of sports magazines and puzzle books. With the remote-control channel changer at her fingertips, and even the telephone plugged in within arm's reach, Stevie had everything a person stuck in bed for a whole week could need.

Everything except two good ankles and some company, Stevie thought angrily.

This was the second day she had missed school. It was the doctor's orders that she should stay off her sprained ankle for at least a week. Stevie didn't mind missing school, but she did mind missing her friends. The time dragged by slowly as she tried hard to find things to do that could be done lying in bed. Even all the extra attention from her mother and brothers, and the extra privileges such as the phone in her room, didn't make Stevie feel any happier. She kept going over and over the accident that she was now sure would keep her out of the final tryouts. She remembered how that big girl had been so close to her. The feeling of being shadowed like that made Stevie feel closed in even in her bed.

41

She threw off the covers just to throw off the feeling. What was it that had happened really, she wondered? All she had done was look up for one second to get a word of encouragement from Dave.

Instead, she had looked up and seen Dave too busy with his *new* interests to look after *her* interests. While he laughed and talked with the girl who was wearing the shirt that was meant for Stevie, Stevie was out on the soccer field getting creamed by the Incredible Hulk! Just the memory of it made Stevie mad all over again.

She looked at the clock. Three o'clock. School would be getting out right now, she thought. Molly and Laura and Meg would be meeting in the hallway outside Mrs. Palmer's and Mrs. Higgle's classrooms. They would probably be discussing what awful thing Mrs. Higgle had done. Laura, poor Laura, for some reason had been the only one of the four to be put in Mrs. Higgle's class. Everyone knew she was the meanest teacher in the school. Make that the meanest teacher in the whole universe! Of course, Laura was a good student and under other circumstances probably would have been the teacher's pet. But Mrs. Higgle didn't have any pets. She treated all the kids the same. Badly. Stevie wished she could be there in that hallway making jokes about Mrs. Higgle the way she always did.

A whole week out of school! she thought to herself. How am I going to stand it? Then out loud she said, "You're not going to stand it, Stevie. You're going to lie down it!" She laughed at her own joke. Feeling a little bit better, she reached for one of the get well cards from the kids in her class at school. Without really looking at it for what would have been about the hundredth time, she flipped it down toward her bad ankle. "There," she snarled at her bandaged foot. "Get well, you stupid ankle!"

Stevie shifted her weight a little in the bed and lifted her good foot straight up in the air. Her soccer ball, which had been resting motionless by her right foot, started to roll down the bed. Quickly she brought her foot down and stopped the ball with her outstretched toes. Just as the ball against her foot was about to make her start feeling even worse about probably losing her chance to play in the last big tryout game, Stevie heard giggling outside her door.

She brightened and called out, "What's so

funny?" She watched as her door slowly opened. There were more giggles outside the door.

"You think it's funny to have a good friend all bandaged up and stuck in bed? I'm suffering in here!" Stevie started moaning and groaning loudly.

More giggles floated in. Stevie watched for the faces of her three friends to peek around the door. Instead, three giant Mylar balloons floated into the room. First came a shiny rainbow-covered balloon, followed by a unicorn on a purple background, and behind that a silver balloon with the face of a fluffy, white kitten on it.

"Surprise!" said Laura, Meg, and Molly all together as they came bursting into Stevie's room. In addition to the balloons, the three girls carried armloads of shopping bags filled with Stevie didn't know what.

"Presents for *me*?" Stevie said, putting her hands up to her face in a look of fake surprise. "Oh, you shouldn't have!"

"We didn't," Meg said matter-of-factly. "The balloons are *it*."

"And your homework," Molly said, dropping a load of books down on the stool with the magazines and puzzle books already on it.

"And our company," added Laura, gently.

"The balloons are fantastic," said Stevie, feeling happier than she'd felt all day. "The homework *you* can keep, but the company *I'll* keep. I missed you guys all day. This is *not* fun!"

"How's your ankle today?" Molly asked. "Any better?"

"Only fatter, maybe," said Stevie, holding up the bandaged foot for all to see. "I think this bandage is making it worse. At least it looks worse."

"Well, happy get well, or whatever," said Laura, handing Stevie the string attached to the unicorn balloon. "Read the note."

For the first time, Stevie noticed that all three balloons had notes attached to the strings. She opened Laura's note, written on Laura's special Friends 4-Ever unicorn stationery. She read it aloud:

Dear Stevie,
   Forget your ankle.
   Forget your pain.
   Just remember that we
   Will always remain
   Friends 4-Ever,

                        Laura

"Now read mine," Meg said before Stevie had a chance to thank Laura. Meg handed Stevie the kitten balloon with her note on her kitten stationery. Stevie cleared her throat in an exaggerated, noisy way. She read:

Dear Stevie,
   Emergency meeting!
   Come one and come all!
   Our great soccer star
   Had a bad fall.
   We'll help you get well
   And back on your feet,
   So that big girl who pushed you
   You'll be sure to beat!
   Be brave, Stevie!

                                        Meg

"Aw, Meg," said Stevie sincerely. "Thanks a lot."

"Don't forget mine," Molly said, handing Stevie her rainbow-covered balloon with the matching rainbow notepaper attached.

Dear Stevie,
 You're the greatest.
 You're the best.
 You stand out far
 From all the rest.
 Get well soon.
 You know we care.
 When you need friends,
 We're 4-Ever there!

        Love,

        Molly

 Stevie looked up from the three notes she held on her lap. Before she could speak, Molly dumped out the contents of one of the shopping bags. Out poured blue and white crepe paper streamers, large sheets of blue oak tag, four rolls of tape, two bottles of white glue, marking pens of all colors, bottles of glitter, and a package of colored construction paper.

"Hey," said Stevie, pushing away the notes and her near-tears moment. "What are we making here? Besides a big mess, I mean?"

The girls laughed, relieved to see Stevie acting a little more like herself again. "It's for my party," Laura explained. "We brought all the stuff over so you could help, too. We're making all the party decorations and all the cheerleading pompons and megaphones."

"This will take your mind off your ankle," Meg said.

"If that's what you're trying to do, then you'd better have a lot more stuff than this," Stevie huffed.

"You asked for it, you got it," Meg said, dumping more things onto the bed. Some of the art supplies landed right on Stevie's bad ankle.

"Aaah!" Stevie winced. "My ankle! I thought you wanted to take my mind off it, not dump a bunch of stuff *on* it!" She reached down to push the things off her foot and rub the soreness away.

"Sorry," said Meg. "I guess I got a little carried away."

"Keep it up and you *will* get carried away." Stevie laughed.

"Well, anyway," Molly said, "the club meeting is at your house today, Stevie."

"Right," said Meg. "I officially call this Friends 4-Ever club meeting to order." She tapped Stevie's night table with her knuckles.

"I move that we start with the pompons," said Laura excitedly.

"I move that we each make our own pompons," Molly added.

"And I can't move at all," said Stevie sarcastically. "So, hand me something."

"Here, you make the megaphones," Meg ordered. "Just cut the oak tag and fold it around into cone shapes."

"That's cinchy," said Stevie, who was good at making practically anything. With no effort at all, she rolled a big piece of oak tag into a cone shape, leaving a small opening at one end through which to shout. She taped the cone together and cut around the bottom to make it flat enough to stand up on its own. "Hello!" boomed her voice through the hole at the small end.

"Let me see that," said Molly, reaching a hand

out. "Let's go, Stevie!" she cheered through the hole.

"Well, it works," said Laura, holding her ears.

The telephone rang, startling all the girls since they weren't used to a phone in Stevie's room. "I'll get it," Stevie screamed out to anyone else who might have been reaching for it somewhere else in the house. She picked up the receiver and said, "Hello?"

Stevie's face suddenly turned bright red as her friends watched her hold the phone out away from her face and pretend to choke. She put the phone back to her mouth and said, "Hold on. I'll get him."

Without covering the phone with her hand, Stevie screeched at the top of her lungs, "David Ames! Telephone!" Dave didn't answer. Stevie reached for the oak tag megaphone she had just made. She put it up to her mouth. "Calling David Ames! Telephone for David Ames! It's a girl!"

"I've got it!" Dave yelled back. Stevie could hear him through the phone and from the kitchen downstairs.

"Yes," smiled Stevie smugly as she hung up

and held up the megaphone. "It *definitely* works!" Now they were all laughing as Stevie started imitating the girl on the phone.

"Hello," said Stevie in a too-breathy voice. "This is Patty. Is David there?" Stevie rolled her eyes upward. "I mean, can you believe she asks for 'David' instead of just plain old Dave like everyone else?"

"What's so strange about that, Stephanie?" Molly giggled to Stevie.

"Why, nothing at all, right, Margaret?" Stevie replied, passing the joke over to Meg.

"Well, aren't we all too, too proper," sniffed Meg in a stiff British accent. They all exploded into bursts of laughter.

The time that had dragged so slowly before her friends arrived, now passed too quickly. The afternoon was over before Stevie knew it. By five o'clock Stevie's room looked like a party room instead of a sickroom. The floor was covered with streamers and megaphones and glittery, cut-out letters saying things such as "Go Team!" and "WIN!" and "Hooray!"

As the girls piled the things back into the shopping bags and started to say their good-byes and see-ya-tomorrows, Stevie held up a surprise. Smiling happily, she showed them all the glittery, cut-out letters she had worked on. *FRIENDS 4-EVER!*

Molly quickly reached for a pair of pompons. Punching the air with one pomponed hand at a time she cried out, "Give me an S!"

"S!" answered Meg and Laura, picking up pompons of their own.

"Give me a T!" Molly shouted.

"T!" came the cheering reply.

"Give me an E!" Molly continued, spelling Stevie's name out letter by letter.

"E!" shouted the girls.

"Give me a break!" Stevie interrupted in a loud, cheering voice of her own. Again they were all swept away by gales of laughter as they punched pompons in front of each other's faces on their way out.

Stevie heard them cheering her all the way down the stairs and out the front door. The sound grew fainter and fainter as the three cheering girls walked farther down the street. When Stevie couldn't hear them at all anymore, she fell back into the mountain of pillows and looked down the bed at her big, fat, swollen ankle. Then she looked up at the three floating balloons which hung over her as a reminder that even if she lost her chance to play in the Select soccer tryouts, she would never lose her friends.

"I THINK I CAN, I THINK I CAN!"

Stevie opened one eye at a time. With the first one opened, she looked down at the end of her bed at the lump that was her ankle under the covers. She opened the other eye and watched the lump to see how much it would move when she tried to bend her ankle. It didn't move much. She looked past her ankle because now that both eyes were opened, a big sign on her door caught her attention. BEWARE OF SISTER! ENTER AT YOUR OWN RISK! read the sign in big black letters.

"Very funny, Dave," she mumbled, as she pulled the covers up and over her head. She knew he was the one who had put the sign there. She also knew why. For the whole week that she'd been stuck in bed, she hadn't been very nice or friendly to Dave. Thanks to him she was missing all the most important things. First her friends, then soccer, then school, and worst of all, Laura's party. If she couldn't even get around her room how was she going to go to a party?

It was all Dave's fault.

Dave had made many tries at being friendly to Stevie. But something would always stop Stevie from being able to forgive him completely for getting her into this awful mess. She had heard somewhere that anger releases some kind of poison into the body. She felt that if that were true she would already have been *completely* poisoned. She was *that* angry.

Sometimes it was hard to stay mad at Dave. Like the day before when he peeked around her doorway with that new smile of his and said, "How ya doin', Stevarino?"

Of course she had said nothing.

"Aw, you're not still mad at me, are ya?" he said.

Still no answer from Stevie.

"Well, do me a favor," he'd finally said, giving up. "When it's safe for me to come in again, hang out a white flag, okay?" Then without waiting for her *not* to answer him again, he bounded down the stairs and rushed out the front door.

Stevie had just been about to soften a little toward him, when she heard Dave's farewell words to their mother.

" 'Bye, Mom," he'd called out. "I'm going to meet Patty after school!" Then the door slammed and he was gone.

As she lay in bed under the covers, Stevie said, *"Patty,"* out loud. "Patty who doesn't even have enough shirts of her own so my brother has to give her *his!"* She had spit out every word as though they were lima beans.

Now, as Stevie peeled back the covers just enough to see the sign again, she set her mouth in a pout. It was Friday morning, another school day for everyone else and another boring day for Stevie Ames. The last good day she'd had was the day Laura, Molly, and Meg came over to make decorations for Laura's party. Since the decorations were made, the three girls had to spend more time at Laura's house, decorating. Stevie, still following the doctor's orders, stayed home and missed out on the fun. The girls dropped by every day to bring Stevie her homework and to try to bring her a little cheer. After five days of it all four girls were a little tired of having to stay in Stevie's room so much. Each day the visits got shorter and shorter. Since this day was the day before Laura's birthday party, Stevie was sure the visit would be just "Hi, goodbye!"

Even good friends aren't good at just sitting around watching another good friend just lie in bed, Stevie thought.

Stevie reached for a piece of her stationery with the blue high-top sneakers in the corners. She might as well write a note to Molly, she guessed. At least writing a letter to Molly would make her feel almost as if she were sitting next to her at school right now. In fact, if she were in her seat in Mrs. Palmer's class, chances are Stevie really would have been writing a note to pass to Molly. She began:

Dear Molly,

Here's a riddle. What has four wheels and flies in summer? A garbage truck! OK, now here's another riddle. What do you get when you cross Stevie Ames? You get her really mad, that's what you get! And that's how I feel about my brother right now. Like he really crossed me. Every time I look at my ankle I get mad at him all over again. It's all because of him and those silly girls. It's all because he gave away the shirt that was supposed to be for me. It's all because now I won't even get to try out for Select. And it's all because I'm having the worst time I've ever had. I can't play soccer. I can't go to school. I can't see my friends whenever I want. I can't . . ."

Suddenly Stevie stopped. "Can't, can't,

can't," she said out loud. "Whew! What is going on with me?" She put down the paper and pen. Next she pulled her bandaged foot out from under the covers and swung it over the edge of the bed alongside the other foot. She could feel a tingling in her foot as the blood rushed through her leg and down into her foot. It hurt at first, but after a few seconds the bad feeling went away. The injured foot felt heavier than the other one, but Stevie realized that the feeling was not pain.

"Hey!" she said in surprise. "It doesn't hurt! My ankle actually doesn't hurt now!" She reached over to the place by her bed where a pair of crutches was leaning against the light blue wall. They were Dave's old crutches, the ones he had used three years before when he fell out of the climbing tree and broke his leg. Stevie remembered how brave Dave had been.

He sure didn't lie around saying, "I can't. I can't," Stevie thought, placing one crutch on each side of herself. Very slowly she stood up, putting all her weight on the right crutch. She kept her bad foot lifted up off the floor and slipped the other crutch under her left arm.

I'm standing by myself! she thought happily.

Putting one crutch in front of the other, Stevie took one step. Then another. Then another. "I think I can," she said determinedly. "I *think* I can." It was the first time since the accident that she was out of bed without someone helping her. She hobbled over to the full-length mirror on the inside of her closet door to take a look at herself.

"Yeecchh!" she said to her reflection. "You look totally disgusting! No wonder no one wants to sit and look at that yucky-looking person!"

Stevie saw herself standing in wrinkled and too-often-worn striped pajamas. Her long hair was matted together in a clump on one side, and stringy on the other. She looked so pale that even her freckles seemed sick. And worst of all was her face. It had an angry, pouty look. Stevie leaned closer to the mirror and stared.

"I think I can," she said. She tried a small smile. The face in the mirror smiled back. She smiled a bigger smile. So did the mirror face. Then she pinched her cheeks, trying to get back a little of the usual pink color. The face in the mirror was looking pinched and pinker, too. Next, she reached for her blue plastic hairbrush and started unmatting the mess. It worked.

Stevie was looking better and better.

All that was left to go were the pajamas. The dresser was all the way across the room. Stevie looked over at it. "I think I can. I think I can," she said, moving one crutch in front of the other until she had clomped her way over to the dresser. Leaning down with the crutch still under her arm, she reached into the drawers and pulled out a pair of zip-leg jeans and her Red Sox sweatshirt. All the while that she worked on getting back to the bed, getting her pajamas off, and getting her clothes on, Stevie kept up her chant of self-encouragement. "I think I can. I think I can. I think I can." She said it so often that she laughed at herself. "Gee, I hope I don't turn into The Little Engine That Could!"

At last, Stevie was dressed for the first time in a whole week! Grabbing the crutches, she stood up and hopped over to the mirror again. "You look mah-valous!" she said to the new girl in the mirror. Then she chanted, "I *thought* I could. I *thought* I could," and she did a very little dance on her crutches.

Stevie spent the next few hours tackling the mountain of work Meg and Molly had brought home from Mrs. Palmer's class. Until now she hadn't felt a bit like doing homework. "Just *being* home is work enough," she had grumbled to her mother when she'd asked Stevie how she was doing on keeping up with her schoolwork. Once Stevie settled her crutches against the side of her desk and settled herself in the chair, keeping her bad ankle propped up on the Red Sox wastebasket under the desk, the work went quickly. By three o'clock in the afternoon, the whole week's worth of homework was done.

Slamming her books closed, Stevie turned in her chair and stretched out both feet in front of her. She saw the soccer ball on the floor next to her bed. Pulling herself up on the crutches, Stevie made her way over to the ball. She opened her closet door so she could see herself in the long mirror. Watching her reflection, Stevie reached out her right foot and gave the soccer ball a swift push-pass kick to the mirror. As the ball reached the mirror, Stevie threw her foot out again so that her reflection could stop the ball. It was a perfect pass and a perfect block. Way to go, Stevie! she cheered to herself. "You've still got what it takes," she said out loud, ignoring the ache that was starting to spread through her bad ankle. She was just getting a little tired, that was all. Maybe she'd better get off her feet for a while, she thought.

Stevie bumped along on her crutches until she reached the wall. She leaned the crutches up against the wall and picked up the timer that was on her desk. She turned the dial and set the timer for 11 minutes 35 seconds, one second over her best headstand record. Then she slowly bent over. Putting her head down on the floor, Stevie brought both legs up over her head. A big smile spread over her face as she realized the happy fact: Even a bad ankle couldn't keep her from doing a perfect headstand! And this was how her three friends found her when they stopped by on their way home from school.

"Hey, Stevie!" Molly's voice called out from the downstairs hallway. "We're here to get you out of that silly old bed!"

"Up and at 'em!" Meg added in her best drill sergeant's voice.

"Rise and shine!" Laura's voice sang out sweetly. All three girls were laughing at their own "toughness" as they ran up the stairs.

"No more of this lazy-bones-lying-around-doing-nothing stuff for you, Stephanie Ames," Molly scolded before she reached the doorway.

All three crowded around the door to Stevie's room, and all three gasped at the sight they saw.

"Stevie!" three voices screamed out in shock.

"What do you think you're doing?" Meg cried.

"You *know* what the doctor said!" Laura exclaimed.

Stevie looked at her three upside-down friends and laughed. "Right! He said stay off my feet. And that's exactly what I'm doing!"

"But you can't . . ." began Molly.

Just then the timer beeped, signaling that Stevie had broken her own record. "Well," said Stevie. "*I* think I *can*!" Bringing her legs slowly down, she righted herself again and reached for her crutches. Smiling her biggest smile, Stevie looked at her friends and said, "I can and I *did*!"

No longer speechless, Molly said, "Nothing can keep you down!"

"And nothing can keep me from Laura's party tomorrow!" Stevie said happily.

"Oh, Stevie, do you really think you can come?" asked Laura hopefully.

Without a minute's hesitation, Stevie simply said, "I definitely think I can!"

LAURA'S PARTY

When Molly and Meg arrived to pick her up, Stevie was already downstairs. In honor of Laura's party, Stevie was dressed in her best jeans and a blue, spatter-painted sweatshirt. Her hair was brushed and pulled back in a ponytail, held by a stretchy, blue terrycloth band.

"You look terrific, Stevie!" said Molly, feeling happy to see her friend out of pajamas two days in a row.

"Check these out," Stevie said, holding up one of her crutches.

"Stevie! You're a genius!" Meg said.

"Another example of your incredible artistic talent," Molly said, sounding as proud as if she'd done the work herself.

On closer look the girls could see that Stevie had painted both crutches blue and white, the colors of Laura's party decorations. On the front of one crutch were the words *Friends 4-Ever! Molly, Stevie, Laura, and Meg!* On the other crutch were the words *Four Cheers for 4 Friends!* Hanging from the top of each crutch was a blue-and-white-streamered pompon. The effect was festive, and Stevie looked ready for what was sure to be one of the best parties ever.

"But before we can go over to Laura's we have to wrap the presents," Meg said. "Wait'll you see what we picked out for her, Stevie."

"Thanks a lot for doing the shopping for me," Stevie said. "What did you get? I can't believe I forgot to even ask yesterday."

"Well, you couldn't anyway because Laura was right there," Molly explained for Stevie. "And we didn't bring it up because we didn't want to ruin the surprise, either."

"Show me!" Stevie said, shifting her weight on the crutches and making the pompons swing as she did.

Molly and Meg pulled two boxes out of the shopping bag they'd carried in with them. One box was a small, pink-velvet box. The other was a big, shiny pink box. Stevie opened the big box first and pulled out a huge beach towel with a giant pair of pink ballet slippers painted on it. The long ribbons flowing down the sides of the towel ended up spelling *LAURA* in beautiful ribbon letters.

"It's gorgeous!" exclaimed Stevie, spreading the towel out with Molly's help. "She'll love it!"

"Okay," said Meg, hurrying to fold it back up and lay it in the pink tissue paper lining the pink box. "That's from all three of us and so is what's next." She closed the box top over the ballet towel, and reached for the smaller box. She handed the velvet box to Stevie.

Hugging the crutches under her arms so that both hands would be free, Stevie held the box gently. The smooth, deep velvet gave a clue that some wonderful treasure was inside this box. Stevie rubbed her fingers across the top of the box, changing the pink to a darker color pink and then back again as she rubbed her fingers back across it.

"Open it!" Molly said breathlessly. "I can't stand the suspense."

"You already know what's in it," Meg laughed.

"I know," Molly answered, "but it's so good I can't wait to see it all over again."

Stevie didn't keep her waiting a minute longer. She snapped open the hinged box and the present was there for everyone to see. "Oh, wow!" Stevie gasped. "She is going to go crazy over this. It's perfect. It's the most perfect Laura present I've ever seen." Stevie lifted out a thin gold chain on which a tiny pair of pink porcelain ballet shoes hung in a permanent perfect *pointe*. Every detail of the necklace was perfect, from the tiny, satiny shoes to the long delicate ribbons that were tied in perfect porcelain bows. The three girls "ooed" and "aahed" over their present for Laura, and passed the necklace around one more time before returning it to its pink padded box.

"You guys really know how to shop!" said Stevie, handing the box back to Meg. "Of course it's not exactly what *I* would have picked out. . . ."

"Yeah, but who besides you would want a

bicycle-tire pump or knee pads for her birth-day?" Meg said sarcastically.

"You're right about that," agreed Stevie. "A bike pump or knee pads in a velvet box wouldn't look so great."

"Not to mention how a bike pump might look on a gold chain!" Meg giggled.

"Well, anyway," Molly stopped them, "enough of that. We have to wrap these things and sign the — "

"Oh, no!" Meg said. "I forgot to get the card!"

"No problem," Stevie said, pulling out the other surprise she had for them. "While I was decorating the crutches I also made a card from all of us!"

"Ballet shoes! How did you know to do that on the front of the card without even seeing the presents we got?" Molly was amazed at Stevie's good guess.

"I'm a genius," joked Stevie. "Just like you said I was." Now they were all laughing together as Meg pulled out two sheets of ballet shoe wrapping paper. While Meg wrapped one present and Molly wrapped the other, Stevie wrote a short poem inside the card for Laura.

Yours 'til the meatball bounces,
Yours 'til the state parks,
We'll be your Friends 4-Ever,
Or at least 'til the dogwood barks!
Happy birthday, Laura!
      Love,

STEVIE *Molly* Meg

"There!" said Meg, holding up the big box, which was now wrapped. "Finished."

"Me, too," Molly added, turning the small box over in her fingers. "This is so small you don't really get to see much of the ballet shoes."

"It doesn't matter," said Stevie. "The shoes inside are the ones to see. Let's go. Is it time?"

"Oh, my gosh!" exclaimed Molly. "You're not kidding it's time. If we don't leave right this second we'll be late!"

"That's all right," Stevie joked. "We can run!" She held up a decorated crutch as she pretended to make a dash for the door.

The girls held her back. "Hey, hold on!" Molly said, touching Stevie's arm. "Don't wreck your ankle all over again just when it's getting better."

"Just kidding," Stevie laughed. "We'll walk."

"Right," said Meg. "And we'd better get going right now."

It was slow going to Laura's house. She only lived down the street and around the corner, on the road the neighborhood was named for, Crispin Landing. But, with one girl on crutches and the other two carrying presents in one hand and trying to help their friend with the other, even a short distance seemed long. At last they made it.

"Whew!" said Stevie, feeling a little worn out after the walk. "My arms get tired. It's hard with these crutches."

Molly rang Laura's doorbell. "I wonder if we're the first ones here. Are you all right, Stevie?"

"Yeah, I'll be okay. I'll sit down when we get inside." Stevie hopped a little on one foot just to get her balance better.

"Shh! Here she comes!" hushed Meg, hiding the present behind her back. Molly did the same with the present she held. Stevie stood behind Molly and Meg trying to hide her crutches. The door opened.

"Happy birthday!" cried Molly, Stevie, and Meg all together.

Laura looked beautiful. Her long, dark hair was in a French braid with blue and white ribbons entwined in the braid. She wore a white sweater and a short blue skirt. Her feet, in bright white leather sneakers and white socks, were ready for plenty of good cheering jumps. On the sweater was a big letter *L* for *Laura* and a blue felt cheering megaphone. "Come on in!" said Laura happily. "Shana and the other two girls from my ballet class are already here. And I have something for all of you." She handed each a letter *L*, a megaphone, and pins. "Pin these on your sweaters or sweatshirts or whatever."

"Here," said Meg, holding out the big box. "We have something for you, too."

"And here," Molly added, handing Laura the small box.

"Oh!" Laura whispered, "how beautiful! I love the paper!"

"And Stevie made the card," Molly said proudly.

"And did you see her crutches?" Meg added. "She decorated them especially for your party."

Stevie held up her blue-and-white crutches and the pompons shook. "Neat, huh?" said Stevie. "I knew I wouldn't be able to do the cheers too well, but at least my crutches are in the spirit of things!"

"They look great!" Laura beamed. "Shana, Cindy, Hilary! Come here and see Stevie's crutches!"

The other three girls came in wearing big letter L's and blue felt megaphones pinned to their sweaters, too. "Incredible crutches, Stevie," said the girl with the black spiky hair.

"Thanks, Shana." Stevie smiled.

"I didn't know you were such a good artist," said the red-haired girl.

"Cindy," said Hilary. "You know she did all the costumes for their class play, remember?"

"Oh, yeah," remembered Hilary. "Well, anyway, your crutches look great."

Before Stevie could say thanks again, Laura hustled them all into the party room. "This way, cheerleaders!" She laughed, leading them into what used to be the dining room but now looked like a gymnasium.

Now Stevie could see what had kept her friends so busy all week. "This is so fabulous!"

she said, looking at the mural they'd painted. There were painted bleachers filled with a crowd of sports fans. There were painted people selling popcorn and hot dogs, and there was even a painted dog eating a hot dog that had fallen on the painted ground.

"Hey!" said Stevie, spying the dog. "It's Riggs!"

"Well," said Molly, "you don't think we could have a party without my beautiful little dog, do you?"

"And my beautiful big fat cat!" added Meg, pointing to a painted orange cat that looked just like Meg's cat Marmalade.

"How'd you do such a great job without me?" asked Stevie only half joking.

"It was ten times as hard, that's all," Molly said.

"Where are the cheerleaders?" Meg asked, suddenly realizing that they were missing.

"Oh, they should be here pretty soon," answered Laura. "I can't wait!"

"So open your presents then," Stevie suggested. "Might as well do the best stuff first!" Everyone laughed as they gathered around Laura and the pile of presents. Laura opened the gifts in the order in which they'd arrived. Shana's present was a boxed set of Laura's favorite book series. Cindy brought a cassette tape of some classical ballet music that Laura loved to dance to. And Hilary brought a new pair of leg warmers for Laura to wear during warm-ups for ballet class. Next, Laura opened the big box from Meg, Molly, and Stevie. When she took out the towel everyone gasped with delight. But the biggest gasps of all came when Laura opened the beautiful pink velvet box and pulled out the pink porcelain shoes on the gold chain.

"Oh, it's beautiful," Laura said breathlessly. She fastened the chain around her neck. "Thank you so much, everyone. All the presents are wonderful." She gave each girl a big hug and when she got to Molly, Meg, and Stevie the hugs were even bigger. Just as she was about to say how much she loved everything for about the hundredth time, the doorbell rang.

"They're here!" shouted all the girls at the same time.

"I have to sit down," Stevie said, feeling suddenly too weak to stand a minute longer on the crutches. She found a chair against the wall in the party room.

Laura ran for the door, but her mother had reached it first. "Hello, girls," said Mrs. Ryder to the cheerleaders. "You look wonderful! I'm glad you could come. I was just in the kitchen finishing up getting the food ready. Laura, honey, why don't you take the girls into the other room, and you can all get started."

All the girls crowded around the two older girls who would be leading the cheers and teaching them all the right moves. "Oh! Are those real pompons?" Stevie heard Molly asking.

"I love your cheerleading outfits!" Stevie heard Laura saying.

"Okay girls," said one of the cheerleaders. "Why don't you all sit down on the floor in front of us, and we'll introduce ourselves." First Laura sat. Then Meg. Then Shana, Hilary, and Cindy. Then Molly. Now Stevie, from where she sat in the chair against the wall, could see the guests of honor for the first time. Her eyes opened wide. Her mouth opened wider.

"Oh, no!" Stevie barely breathed.

"I'm Patty," said one of the girls whose hair was styled and stiffened just enough with a small amount of mousse.

"And I'm Jill," said the other girl, smiling out

at Stevie's friends with her blue eyes gently shaded in just the tiniest bit of purple shadow.

"We're going to show you some of the best cheers. Then after we show you how we do them, you can show us how you do them." Patty and Jill both did a quick little jump, bringing their feet together as they clapped a quick, loud clap.

"Hey!" they both shouted together. "Open your eyes! Open your ears! Here comes the team with all the cheers!" As they screamed these words out in a peppy-sounding chant, they did some kind of jumping step that Stevie couldn't quite see through the blur of tears that now scalded her eyes.

It was *them*! The two girls who had come to her house that day. The same two who had come to her soccer tryouts, not to see *her* but to see Dave! The exact same two girls who had taken Dave away from her. And one of them had even taken Dave's shirt! Stevie felt suddenly sick. She started to stand, but the decorated crutches had somehow been knocked over and now lay too far out of reach. The pompons on the crutches were as crushed as Stevie was.

"Molly!" Stevie called out in a loud whisper.

But Molly couldn't hear. She was already caught up in the screaming of "Open your eyes! Open your ears! Here comes the team with all the cheers!" In fact, now Stevie saw that all the girls were involved in the cheering. They were all trying to copy every move the two older girls made. If the two girls jumped, Laura, Meg, Molly, Shana, Cindy, and Hilary jumped. If they shouted, the rest of them shouted. No one seemed to notice or care about the moussed-up hair or the purple eye shadow. No one seemed at all concerned about the fact that these two girls were almost single-handedly responsible for Stevie's accident. And no one seemed to notice or care about Stevie and her fallen crutches right now.

"Open your eyes! Open your ears!" all the girls except Stevie shouted.

No one seemed to notice or care when Stevie quietly picked up her blue-and-white crutches, sneaked out of the party room, and headed slowly for home.

GOOD NEWS,
GREAT NEWS

The walk home from Laura's party seemed a lot longer to Stevie than the walk there. It also seemed a lot lonelier. Sneaking away, even on crutches, was easy. All the girls were so busy cheering and jumping and shouting and copying every little thing the two cheerleaders were doing, they didn't hear Stevie's crutches thumping toward the front door. They didn't hear the door open and they didn't hear it close behind Stevie.

And they probably hadn't even noticed yet that I'm gone! Stevie thought bitterly. She walked briskly, throwing one crutch in front of the other and hopping hard on the one good foot. As she walked, the blue-and-white pom-poms on the crutches shook and brushed roughly against her. It was as if they were trying to remind Stevie of the cheering that was going on back at the party. After about two more shakes and brushes Stevie reached across to the right crutch and ripped off the pompon. She did the same to the one on the other side. Crumpling up the streamers, Stevie dropped them into an open garbage can that some neighbor hadn't brought into the garage yet.

"A perfect dunk!" Stevie said out loud, pretending the streamers were a well-aimed basketball and the can was the hoop. "And the crowd goes wild as Stevie Ames scores again, bringing her team to victory!" Stevie's best sports announcer voice echoed up the street with no one to hear it except some robins who were building a nest in Stevie's favorite climbing tree. One of the birds sang something back to Stevie.

"Well, at least *someone* appreciates me!" Stevie said, looking up into the branches of the big tree. "Or maybe that just means my basketball playing is for the birds." Her own jokes were making her slow down a little. She started walking without throwing the crutches ahead of herself. When she got to the tree she stopped. How long had it been since she'd been up in the tree? No one could climb as high as Stevie Ames, not even her brothers. For a minute Stevie thought she might just throw the crutches aside and climb to the highest branch, ankle or no ankle. The same bird chirped a warning to her.

"Okay, okay," said Stevie to the bird. "It was just a thought." Just as she was about to walk on, Stevie noticed a rainbow peeking out of a crack in the tree. It was Molly's rainbow stationery. Stevie reached for it and saw that the ink was smeared. It had been stuck in the tree for a while, she guessed, and the morning dew must have gotten it damp. She carefully unfolded the note. Even with the smeared ink, Stevie could still read it easily.

Dear Stevie,

No rhyme this time (whoops! that was an accident). I know you won't find this note until your ankle is all better. But just because you're stuck in bed it doesn't mean a note can't be stuck in the secret note spot. When you read this it will mean that you are back on your feet again. And that will mean that you are feeling better. And that will mean that I'm feeling better. If you feel bad, I feel bad. So remember, Stevie. Try to feel good so I do, too.

Yours 'til the Square Dances,

Molly

Stevie folded the note up again and stuffed it into her jeans pocket. She started to settle the crutches under her arms again and walk on, but instead she read Molly's note one more time. *If you feel bad, I feel bad*, it read.

Then she must be feeling bad right now, Stevie thought. No sooner did she have that thought than Molly appeared running toward Stevie.

"Hey, Stevie," Molly called out. "Where'd you go?"

"Home, almost," Stevie answered, feeling a little ashamed of herself for leaving and making Molly leave, too, to come after her. "My ankle was bothering me, and I didn't want to spoil the party." She couldn't look Molly in the eye.

"Stevie Ames, do you think that just because I was away in Kansas so long I don't know you anymore?" Molly stood with her hands on her hips, blocking Stevie's path home.

"What do you mean?" Stevie asked, even though she knew exactly what Molly meant.

Instead of looking as if she felt sorry for Stevie with her bad ankle and all, Molly looked mad. "What I mean is I don't think you left because of your ankle. I think you left because of those cheerleaders."

Molly was talking very fast, and Stevie was startled by her friend's tone of voice. "At first I didn't realize who they were," Molly continued.

"Then I remembered that day in your room when we were all making decorations. When you were imitating the girl who called your brother you said her name was Patty." Molly took a deep breath. "So, the Patty at the party is the same Patty who called Dave. So?"

"So what," Stevie shot back.

"So that's why you left. Tell the truth, am I right?" Molly's eyes flashed.

"So, what of it?" Stevie said. Now she was mad, too.

"So what about Laura? And what about the party? And what about Meg and me? And what about how we all feel?" Molly stamped her foot as she spoke.

"How *do* you all feel?" Stevie snapped back at Molly. "I'm the one who's left out of everything because of that stupid girl talking to my stupid brother at that stupid soccer game. And now she's at Laura's party, and — "

"And *we're* not?" said Molly. "It's Laura's special day today, and we should both be there cheering for her instead of here screaming at each other."

"Then you go back," said Stevie. "I have nothing to cheer about, anyway."

"Stevie Ames, today the cheering should be for Laura, and I'm going back to do just that!" Molly spun around and stomped all the way back to the party. Stevie was left standing alone. In her anger, Stevie dropped the rainbow note on the ground. Without thinking, she lifted her bad ankle up and gave the note a swift kick.

Suddenly Stevie realized what she had just done. She had just kicked Molly's note with her bad ankle and *it hadn't hurt*! "Hey!" she called out to nobody. "It didn't hurt! It didn't hurt a bit!" She looked up the street and saw Molly just going in to Laura's house. "Hey, Molly!" she started to call out. But then she remembered Molly was mad at her. Instead of following Molly, Stevie turned and headed for home. When she got to her door, her mother was waiting for her.

"Mom!" Stevie said with surprise. "What are you doing just standing at the door?" Stevie noticed a funny look on her mother's face.

"I just called Laura's mother, and she said you'd left the party. They thought your ankle must have been bothering you too much to stay."

"It was," Stevie said, keeping her eyes down.

"But I saw how you were kicking that foot out all the way down the street. You look pretty good to me." Then her mother seemed to realize that there was something else the matter with Stevie. "Are you just feeling a little down, Stevie Lou?"

"Oh, I'm all right," Stevie answered, not ready to blurt out the fact that she'd just had a terrible fight with her best friend in the whole world.

Now Dave and Mike came to the door. They had the same funny look on their faces as their mother did. "What are you guys up to?" grumbled Stevie, remembering that if it hadn't been for Dave and that girl Patty, she might still be at the party and her best friend would still be her best friend.

"Hey, Stevarino," said Dave, grinning the widest grin Stevie had ever seen on his face. "Guess what I have here?" He held up a white envelope and dangled it teasingly through the doorway and in front of her face.

"A white envelope, big deal," said Stevie without any curiosity.

"And what do you think is *in* that white envelope?" Mike taunted.

"A million dollars," joked Stevie.

"Better," said Dave.

"Much better," said Mike.

"A best friend who isn't mad at me?" Stevie said softly.

"Come in, Stevie," said her mother, opening the door wider to allow for the crutches. Now she was smiling that funny smile even more.

"Well, then what is it?" Stevie asked, feeling tired of this game. "If it's a million dollars for me, I'm quitting my paper route."

Dave, Mike, and Stevie's mother couldn't hold the surprise in a minute longer. "You made it, Stevie!" shouted Dave, waving the white envelope through the air high above his head. "You made the finals! I know we shouldn't have opened your letter, but we couldn't wait!"

"That's what's in the envelope," Mike explained excitedly. "It's the letter saying you made it!"

"I did?" Stevie said slowly and quietly. Then louder, "I did? You mean I really did! Don't just say it if it isn't true." Then she looked at her mother's face, which was beaming with pride, and she knew for sure they weren't just saying it. Stevie took the envelope from her brother's hand and read the letter silently. "I made it," she barely whispered, looking up at Dave.

Dave ruffled her hair the way he always did. "You sure did, Stevarino," he said. "Just like I knew you would."

"There was no way you couldn't make it with two of the best coaches in the world helping you," bragged Mike. "I knew you'd make it, too."

"And I have even better news than that," added Stevie, brightening for the first time since she'd left the party.

"What's that?" asked Dave.

Kicking her bandaged ankle out in front of her and feeling no pain, Stevie said, "My ankle made it *with* me!" Everybody laughed as Stevie swung the ankle back and forth.

"This calls for a celebration!" her mother said happily.

"Yeah," Stevie said, remembering what Molly had said in their fight. "And there's one going on right now. See ya later." Stevie handed the letter to her mother and turned to go out the door.

"Where are you going?" her mother asked.

"Back to Laura's party," Stevie said.

"Well, don't you want to bring the letter with

you so you can share your good news?" Dave asked, holding the letter up.

Stevie stopped for a minute and thought. Then looking back at Dave, her mother, and Mike, she smiled and said, "Naa, I won't tell them today. Today is Laura's day. See ya." Stuffing Molly's note back into her jeans pocket, Stevie hurried back to the party. She arrived just in time to see Laura make a wish and blow out the candles on her cake. When all the candles were out in one blow, Meg, Molly, and Stevie cheered.

"What did you wish?" Meg asked. "You *have* to tell."

"I wished that the Friends 4-Ever would really be friends *forever*," Laura answered, licking some icing off her fingers.

Holding both crutches under one arm, Stevie put her other arm around Molly's shoulders. The two girls smiled at each other. "That's one wish," Stevie said, "that's sure to come true."

GUESS WHO'S BACK?

When the morning bell rang in Crispin Landing Elementary School, the crowd that was gathered around Stevie didn't go running to their class-rooms. It was Stevie's first day back at school and all the kids from Mrs. Palmer's class and Mrs. Higgle's class were anxious to see for them-selves if Stevie's ankle really was better. It was. The crutches were gone, and Stevie was walking with her weight on both feet. The bad ankle still felt a little weak, but the doctor had said it was all right for her to start back to school.

Everyone wanted to hear about the accident

firsthand from Stevie. They wanted to know who that big girl was. How did it happen? Did it hurt really bad? How was her great week off from school? And most of all everyone wanted to congratulate Stevie on making the final tryouts for Select soccer. Stevie wasn't just the only *girl* from Crispin Landing Elementary who had tried out. She was the only *person* from their school who had made the finals. The whole school was counting on Stevie to represent them on the Select team.

"Can you still kick a ball?" one boy asked.

"Will you be able to run fast enough?" another boy asked.

"Will you be able to play at all?" asked a girl.

"And will you be able to go to your classrooms *now*?" asked a stern Mrs. Higgle. Mrs. Higgle's voice did the job the bell couldn't. Everyone scattered. As the second bell was ringing, both classes made their way to their rooms with Laura sadly saying good-bye to Stevie, Molly, and Meg as they walked toward Mrs. Palmer's class together.

"See you after prison," Stevie said sympathetically to Laura just before Mrs. Higgle shut the door in her face.

The door opened again. "And there will be no more talk like that, Miss Ames, sprained ankle or no sprained ankle!" Mrs. Higgle slammed the door for a second time right in Stevie's face.

"Sheesh!" exclaimed Stevie loudly. "It's a good thing I'm not sensitive!" She said this as she backed into Mrs. Palmer's classroom. As she turned around to find her seat next to Molly and behind Meg, Stevie found something else.

"Surprise!" everyone yelled.

The room was decorated with streamers and confetti. Balloons floated next to each chair. On the blackboard in the front of the room big letters written in colored chalk declared *Welcome Back, Stevie!* And the rest of the board was filled in with funny messages and the signatures of everyone in the class.

"Gee," said Stevie in disbelief, "if I'd known there would be a party I would have come back sooner!"

Mrs. Palmer laughed as she gave Stevie a big hug. "Well, we're glad you're back now," she said. "And I understand you have some other good news. You made the final tryouts for Select soccer! That's wonderful! We're all so proud of you, Stevie."

"Well, I made the finals, but I still have a long way to go before I make the team," Stevie explained.

"That's to think about another day," Mrs. Palmer said. "Today we're just celebrating the fact that you're back and you're back on your feet again."

After the party with doughnuts and orange juice, the rest of the day went by quickly for Stevie. It felt good to be back at school. Being back meant being back with her friends again, but it also meant being back on the soccer field. And that's exactly where she was every day of that week.

On Friday, just as the last bell of the day was about to ring, Meg passed notes to Stevie and Molly. Both slips of paper said the same thing: *Don't forget the club meeting at my house after school!*

The bell rang and the girls were free to talk out loud. "Oh, Meg," said Stevie. "I forgot there was a meeting. I told my brother I'd meet him at the field after school."

"But Stevie," said Molly, stuffing her books into her pink backpack. "You've been meeting him every day. You've missed every meeting this week! We want to start planning the pet wash."

"We were just waiting for Laura's party to be done so we could concentrate on our next thing," Meg added.

"But *my* next thing is the finals tomorrow. I *have* to practice. But I'll come to the next meeting, I promise, and you can put me down for any of the jobs nobody else wants." Stevie hoped her friends were going to be understanding, but they both looked disappointed.

"Is soccer everything to you, Stevie Ames?" Meg demanded unreasonably. "It sure seems like it. It seems like you like soccer more than you like us."

"Hey, wait a minute," Stevie argued. "I like soccer, but I *like* you guys, too. Just because I'm doing soccer right now it doesn't mean I don't still feel the same way about you."

Just then Laura appeared in the doorway. "Well," she said sarcastically, "I've been paroled. I got off for good behavior, which is the only kind of behavior a person can have in Mrs. Higgle's class!"

The girls all laughed, and Stevie was glad that Laura's jokes took the attention away from the discussion about soccer versus best friends. "Are we all ready for the club meeting?" asked Laura, not realizing that *all* of them weren't going.

"Stevie has soccer practice," Molly said.

"Again," Meg added, sounding annoyed.

"Well, after soccer season is over we'll get back to our normal meeting schedule," Laura said with some understanding. It wasn't so long ago that she had missed a lot of meetings because of her ballet recital rehearsals. Before that rehearsals for the class play had kept her from the Friends 4-Ever club meetings. She shifted her purple backpack to her other arm. "Ready?" she asked.

"As we'll ever be," said Meg, leading the way out the door.

Molly followed next to Stevie. "Well, at least you can walk with us partway," she said. "Half a walk is better than none."

"Well, that's the truth." Stevie laughed. "Since I was not walking at all last week!" She picked up her blue backpack. "Ugh! This thing weighs a ton. I forgot I have my soccer cleats and shin guards in here. And the ball, too."

"Any room in there for your books?" Molly joked.

"Oh, books?" said Stevie. "Gee, I guess books would be a good idea." Then she laughed. "Of course I have books in here, too. Soccer isn't *everything*."

Meg and Molly looked at each other and laughed at Stevie. "Oh, *really*?" said Meg.

"Really," said Stevie, putting an arm on Meg's shoulder.

The four girls left the school the way they often did, walking four across and doing a skip step as though they were "off to see the Wizard, the wonderful Wizard of Oz." When they reached the soccer field at the junior high school, Stevie dropped out of the line. "Well, I'll see you guys later," she said, feeling a little sad not going with them.

Soccer *wasn't* everything. Really. And it was hard to watch her friends walk away from her. Really. But secretly Stevie had to admit that spending every day after school with Dave, getting all his attention, was great. Really. She was just thinking about how great it was when she felt a slap on the back.

"Guess who's back?" Dave's voice came up behind her.

Stevie whirled around, but still didn't see Dave because he followed her around. Quickly she turned the other way and was too fast for him.

She slapped him hard on his back and shouted, "*Your* back!"

Stevie threw her heavy bag down on the ground and ran, favoring her right foot. All week her left foot had felt fine, but she was still in the habit of keeping some of her weight off it. As she ran she hopped every other step and got way ahead of Dave. He threw his books down next to Stevie's bag and raced after his sister. He caught up to her quickly and grabbed her by her braided hair.

"Ouch!" screamed Stevie, slowing to a halt. "I give up! Let go of my hair!"

"Ready for practice?" He held her braids tighter. "Say yes," he said, gripping the hair harder.

"Yes! Yes!" Stevie laughed. Dave let go and she ran for her bag. She dumped out her cleats and shin guards and quickly put them on. The ball rolled out and Stevie gave it her best kick.

"Good one, Stevie!" Dave called after her as she ran for the ball. "Keep it going as straight as you can. Remember there's going to be a guard trying to block kicks like that."

At the mention of the guard, all the memories of the accident came back. She had just stolen the ball from that big girl. The girl had caught up and bumped Stevie. That was when she had looked up and seen that Dave's attention was all on Patty and Jill instead of on her. Next thing she knew, she was on the ground, flattened by the weight of the guard. Stevie shuddered at the memory. She got to where the ball was and leaned down to pick it up. When she turned to run back across the field to where Dave was waiting, Stevie couldn't believe her eyes. She thought she had shaken the memory off, but now she was seeing the same sight all over again. Standing across the field, Dave was laughing and talking to those same two girls *again!* The only thing different was that this time they were wearing their cheerleading outfits.

Stevie saw one of the girls, Patty, hand some package to Dave. Presents? Stevie thought to herself. Now she's giving him presents! Stevie felt a stab of jealousy.

Stevie couldn't hear what Dave and the two girls were saying, but she could see they were doing a lot of laughing. Dave waved at Stevie and called out to her. "Hey, Stevie! Come on over here!"

The two girls waved at her, too. "Hi, Stevie!"

called out Patty. "You sure kicked that ball far."

So, Stevie thought, now she's trying to be nice. Well, she doesn't fool me. Stevie ran toward her brother and the two girls, but stopped before she got to them. She picked up her backpack and stuffed the soccer ball into it. Now the other girl, Jill, called out to her.

"Hi, Stevie. We missed you at the party. We were hoping to get to know you a little better there." The girl smiled a white, even smile. For a split second Stevie actually thought the girl looked pretty nice. "Dave said you'd be practicing today, so we thought we'd come see how you're doing now that your ankle is better."

Oh, sure, Stevie thought. Trying to butter me up. Well, it won't work! She stuffed the books that had fallen out of her backpack back into it.

"It's so great that you might be the first girl to make Select soccer," said Patty.

"I always wanted to try out, but I didn't have the nerve," Jill said. "We'll be rooting for you."

"Don't bother!" snapped Stevie angrily. She changed her shoes, gathered all of her stuff together, and started running away.

"Where are you going?" Dave called after her.

"Crazy!" Stevie yelled back without stopping

or turning around. "And *you* can't come!" When she got far enough away that she couldn't hear Dave's voice calling after her, Stevie slowed down. She was panting from running.

"Why did he have to ruin everything?" she cried out loud. And why did *I* have to run away? she scolded herself, stamping her right foot in anger. She wasn't sure who she was more mad at: Dave, those girls, or herself. Suddenly she just felt mixed up. The girls she hated seemed too nice to hate. She wished they'd never talked to her. Then, Stevie knew exactly what to do. Instead of going in the direction of her own house, Stevie turned toward Meg's house.

If I hurry, she thought, maybe I can get there before the meeting is over. She started to run again, anxious to be with the ones she could always count on when she was feeling the way she was feeling now. Even carrying her heavy bag, Stevie reached Meg's house quickly. As the Friends 4-Ever always did on meeting days at Meg's house, Stevie just opened the door and walked in. She headed upstairs to Meg's room. The door was closed, but Stevie was relieved to hear giggles and laughter coming from Meg's room.

Good, said Stevie to herself. They're still here. At least *something* is going right today." She gave a quick two-knuckle knock on Meg's door and then she opened it. The giggles stopped, and Stevie stood with her mouth wide open. Instead of finding her friends sitting on the floor making plans for the pet wash, she found all three of them standing in a chorus line. They wore matching short white skirts, bulky blue pullover sweaters, white socks, and sneakers. In their hands each held a set of blue-and-white cheerleading pompons. And all three looked just like the two girls she had just run away from.

"Stevie!" said Molly, surprised to see her there.

"What are you doing here?" asked Meg, as though maybe Stevie didn't have the right to be there.

"We thought you had soccer practice," Laura said.

"And I thought *you* had a club meeting!" Stevie shouted. "How would I know that my best friends would turn into *this* when I'm not around?" Before anyone could explain anything to her to try to stop her, Stevie turned and ran down the stairs. All she wanted to do was get out and get home.

Stevie ran all the way from Meg's house on Doubletree Court to her own on Half Moon Lane. When she got there, Dave was already home.

"Well, guess who's back," he said when she came running in the house.

This time Stevie didn't stop to joke. She ran up the stairs, into her room, slamming the door behind herself.

At first she just stomped back and forth from one side of her room to the other. Next she picked up the crutches she hadn't used all week and stomped around some more letting them carry her full weight as she lifted herself up and swung her legs forward. As she fumed and stomped and swung and stomped some more, Stevie was thinking. She was thinking about Dave. She was thinking about those two girls. She was thinking about her three best friends. She was thinking about herself. She stopped stomping, sat down on her bed, and thought for a long time.

Then she opened her desk drawer and rummaged around until she found her favorite pen and a piece of her Friends 4-Ever stationery. She clipped the paper to her clear clipboard with her name engraved at the top, and she began her letter to Molly.

Dear Molly,

My ankle is better so how come I don't feel better? I think I know why. It all started when those two girls came looking for my brother. I was feeling so jealous of them. I guess I just didn't want to share him with anyone. It's kind of like how you and Meg might have been feeling about sharing me with soccer. But anyway, I was so mad at everyone that I wasn't even having fun with my brother when he was with me. And because I was mad at him it made me act mad at everyone. Now I'm just mad at myself. You said today that "Half a walk is better than none." But when it comes to friend-

ships, I don't want half a friendship. I want the whole thing. Will you forgive me for acting the way I've been acting? If you will, then my ankle and my feelings will be better.

Friends 'til the Ocean Waves,

STEVIE

GIVE US AN S!

Stevie woke up half an hour before her alarm
clock was set to ring. On the most important day
of her life she sure didn't need an alarm clock
to wake her up. Even though she was awake,
she didn't want to get out of bed just yet. She
liked lying there in the darkness of the early
morning, looking at the sports stars on the post-
ers that hung around her room. She stared for
a very long time at the soccer player. It seemed
as if he were staring back at her. After a few
minutes Stevie almost thought she saw him
move. She blinked her eyes. He moved again!

"What is going on here?" she wondered aloud, hoping the sound of her own voice would take some of the creepiness out of the feelings she was having. Suddenly she laughed and sat up in bed. Now she saw it more clearly. He *was* moving. In fact, the whole poster was moving, but it was because of the heating vent on the floor right under the poster. The morning blast of warm air blew up and under the poster, causing it to ripple slightly.

"Whew!" said Stevie. "I must be more nervous about today than I thought!"

She fell back against her pillow and breathed out, blowing some long strands of hair out of her face. As she settled into her pillow, her thoughts turned back to the day before. She wondered now if Molly had gotten her note. She hoped she would get it before the game. All three of her friends had called after she left Meg's house, but Stevie hadn't been ready to talk to them. She wanted time to sort out her feelings and write the letter to Molly. Now that it was a new day, she did feel like talking to all of them. She needed them to help her get through the tryouts.

Stevie looked at her clock. She still had some

time before the alarm, so she turned in her bed and picked up the photograph of Dave from her night table. The morning sunlight was just starting to spill into her room through the crack between the shade and the window. Some of the light spilled onto the photograph. The red shirt Dave wore looked so bright in the light. Stevie quickly put the framed Dave back on the table. The last thing she wanted to do was start feeling mad at Dave or anyone else this morning.

So what if he forgot that he promised to give me that Winning Shirt if I made the Select team? Stevie thought. And so what if he gave it to that girl, Patty? Maybe she isn't too, too bad after all if Dave likes her.

Stevie picked Dave up again and held him out in front of her. "I forgive you!" she said dramatically to his face. Then, before she put it down again she added, "Well, I'm *trying* to, anyway."

"*Brrriiiinnnngggg!*" the alarm clock blared out.

"Okay, okay," said Stevie as she pushed the button to turn it off. "I hear you. I'm way ahead of you." A minute later she heard the alarm clocks going off in other rooms in the house. In fact, Stevie wasn't the only one having a conversation with a clock this morning.

"Hey!" Dave shouted at his alarm. "Give it a rest, will ya?"

"Ugh!" Mike growled sleepily at his alarm. "Are you kidding me?"

"Stevie! Dave! Mike! Time to get up!" their mother called to them instead of talking to a clock that wasn't going to answer her, anyway.

"I'm up!" Stevie called back, still lying in her bed.

"Ditto," Dave yelled from his room.

"Almost," Mike yawned.

Since Dave's room was right next to her's, Stevie could hear him get up, open and close a few dresser drawers as he pulled out the clothes for the day, and a few minutes later he hurried down the stairs.

I wonder what he's in such a rush about? Stevie thought. I'm the one who should be rushing, I guess. But she felt that if she moved slowly she might make herself believe that she wasn't so nervous. She was acting calm just to fool herself into believing she *was* calm. She waited until Mike and her mother were downstairs, too. Finally she swung her legs over the side of the bed and started to stand up. A sharp pain shot through her left foot. "Ouch!" cried Stevie, sitting back down quickly. Suddenly all her false calm feelings turned to real feelings of panic. "Dave!" she screamed out.

"He's not here," her mother called up the stairs.

"Mom!" Stevie called, feeling a double dose of panic upon hearing that her brother wasn't even there. "My ankle!"

Mrs. Ames came running up to Stevie's room to see what was the matter with her. She found Stevie sitting on the bed, leaning over and rubbing her ankle.

"I just stood up and it killed me," Stevie explained. "I can't put my weight on it." Tears were starting to blur her vision. "Mom, this can't be happening! Not today of all days."

"Now wait a minute," said Mrs. Ames firmly. She bent down on the floor next to Stevie's foot and began to gently rub it. "You probably just have a muscle cramp from all the running you did yesterday." She rubbed some more and slowly turned the foot from one side to the other.

"I think that's helping," Stevie said with relief in her voice. She stood up again, slowly this time. She felt afraid when she leaned on the bad foot, but this time there was no sharp pain. It didn't hurt at all. Stevie hugged her mother and wiped the tears from her own eyes. Now that the pain was gone, Stevie remembered that Dave was gone, too.

"He had something to do first thing this morning," Stevie's mother explained.

"With Patty and Jill?" Stevie asked, trying not to sound jealous.

"Well, he did say something about meeting the girls," Mrs. Ames reported matter-of-factly. "But don't worry. He'll be at the game. Nothing could keep him from it."

There wasn't time for Stevie to think any more about Dave or Dave's girls or anything except just getting herself ready and over to the field. She hurried into her soccer clothes, ate a light breakfast, and was ready to leave. Her mother drove her to the field this time, and even for the short car ride Mike gave Stevie some last-minute tips.

"Watch who's guarding you," he told Stevie. "Try to figure out which side is his strong side, then play to the other side of him."

"If it *is* a him," Stevie said nervously. "It might be a her again, a *big* her." Stevie twisted her fingers together as she recalled the size of the girl who had crushed her ankle.

As the car pulled up to the junior high school, Stevie could see that the field area was already crowded with people who had come to watch. This time, of course, there weren't so many players. Only the best of the best would be playing in this game.

"I'll let you two off here," said Mrs. Ames. "I'll park the car and meet you over there."

Stevie and Mike got out together and walked over to the field. Both of them realized as they looked around at the other players that all of them were the star players on their own teams. The competition was going to be the toughest Stevie had ever had. She was just thinking that thought when she saw the one thing she hoped she wouldn't see. It was the big girl, and she was wearing a uniform. She had made the finals, too.

"Oh, no," moaned Stevie to Mike. "Just when I thought it was safe to go back on the field!"

Mike saw what Stevie saw. "The Return of the Crusher!" he said, as though he were announcing a new movie.

"I think I can. I think I can. I think I can,"

Stevie chugachugged under her breath.

"Can what?" asked Mike.

"Live through this game," Stevie said sarcastically. She nervously looked around for Molly, Laura, and Meg. She didn't see them anywhere. And for that matter, where was Dave? Stevie knew they couldn't have forgotten the game, but did they forget what time it started? In five minutes the whistle would be blowing, and the game would be beginning.

"You'd better hurry over to check in," Mike warned Stevie.

Stevie looked over to where the registration table was set up. Mike gave her a high-five and wished her luck before Stevie ran to let the officials know she was there.

"Hey! Stevie Ames!" said the same man who had been sitting behind the table at the preliminary tryouts. "It's good to see you back. You had some bad luck last time, but that can't happen twice now, can it?" He laughed. She didn't. The thought of getting crushed again wasn't funny to her.

Stevie looked around once again hoping to see her friends and her brother. She saw that her mother had found Mike, and the two of them had a good spot on the sidelines. But still the others she looked for were missing. The whistle blew, calling all players onto the field. As she ran to her position, Stevie could hear her mother's voice cheering her on. It was nice to hear her mother, but she wanted to hear some other voices, too. How could her best friends forget her like this? she wondered.

The whistle blew again, forcing Stevie to turn her attention to the field and away from the sidelines.

"Hey, Ames," said a voice behind Stevie.

Stevie whirled around and was face to face with "the Crusher."

"Today," snarled the big girl, "it's just *you* and *me*."

Stevie didn't have a chance to answer back. The game began and her team had the ball. A boy who reminded Stevie of the soccer player on her poster kicked the ball straight down the field. Another player received it and passed it over to a player who was positioned directly in front of the goal.

"Kick it in! Kick it in!" screamed the people on the sidelines. Stevie's teammate did as he was told. The first goal was scored, and Stevie jumped up and down, cheering her own team.

"Don't get too happy too soon," snapped the big girl, who tightened her guard over Stevie.

Stevie ignored her, or at least tried to. Having the girl hanging over her just like in the last game made Stevie feel a little shakey. She was afraid of getting hurt again. Then the ball came right to her. Stevie acted fast. She started to dribble it down toward the goal, but the girl reached a foot out and stole the ball from Stevie. Now the ball was heading for Stevie's goal. If the big girl scored it was going to be all Stevie's fault, she thought. She ran after the girl and the ball, but she was too late. The big girl was good. She wove in and out of all the players who tried to block her and went right for the goal. She scored and it was the end of the first quarter.

Stevie didn't join the rest of the players who were gathered around the bag of orange slices and the bottled water, which was there to cool them off during the breaks. She felt too bad about allowing the girl to steal the ball and score. So far she was sure she didn't have a chance of making Select. Why would they choose someone who couldn't even keep the ball?

The second quarter began, and once again

Stevie was shadowed by the same hulking guard. If Stevie moved left, the girl moved left. If Stevie turned, the girl turned. If Stevie stopped, the girl moved back and forth frantically in front of Stevie like a moth around a streetlight. And instead of just guarding Stevie, the girl talked to her, trying to make her nervous.

"You'll never get that ball again," hissed the girl. "Your playing days are over after this day."

That did it. Stevie had taken all she was going to take. The boy who looked like her poster had the ball and passed it over to Stevie. Stevie's feet moved like magic, carrying the ball down the field. The girl followed close behind and bumped against Stevie. Suddenly Stevie started having the feeling that what happened before was about to happen again. Fear made her start to lose control of the ball. The girl was closer and closer, reaching her foot out toward the ball. As panic started to overtake Stevie, she heard her name being called from somewhere on the sidelines.

"Go, Stevie!" one voice shouted.

"Take that ball all the way!" another voice shouted.

"You can do it, Stevie!" a third voice shouted.

It was Molly, Laura, and Meg, screaming as loud as they could for their friend.

Stevie didn't look over at them. She never took her eyes off the ball. But hearing their voices screaming, "Give us an S, give us a T, give us an E, and a V-I-E!" gave Stevie all the extra strength and courage she needed to keep the ball and herself away from the crushing shadow of the big girl on the other team. From that moment on, the game was Stevie's. She scored, she made perfect passes so others on her team could score, and she never lost control of the ball.

At halftime, Stevie looked for her friends. Now, even in the crowd of people it was easy to spot them. Standing in a line, Molly, Meg, and Laura stood dressed in matching short white skirts, bulky blue sweaters, and white socks and sneakers. In their hands each held a set of blue-and-white cheerleading pompons. Stevie didn't feel mad this time when she saw them dressed that way. And she didn't even feel mad when she saw two other cheerleaders, Patty and Jill, leading her friends in cheers and jumps especially for Stevie Ames.

For the rest of the game the other team didn't

have a chance. The Friends 4-Ever cheerleaders gave Stevie's whole team a burst of energy that the other team was never able to hold down. When the game was over, and Stevie's team had won, the crowd screamed and cheered louder than ever before. And when the announcements were made of the names of those players chosen for the Select soccer team, Stevie Ames was the first and only girl to make the team.

Now her cheerleading friends, her mother, and Mike all ran onto the field to hug Stevie and congratulate her. Stevie thought she could never feel happier than she did at that moment.

And then Dave came over to her. "Hey, Stevarino," he said proudly, ruffling her hair as usual.

"Dave! Where were you?" Stevie asked, too happy to be mad that she hadn't seen him for the whole game.

"I was watching every move you made, Stevie. But I didn't want you to see me. The only thing I wanted *you* to see was that you could do it all by yourself." He put his arm around her and pulled something out of his jacket. Stevie could see that it was the same package she'd seen Patty handing to him the day before.

"What's that?" Stevie asked.

"Open it up and look for yourself," said Dave, handing the package to her.

Stevie opened the package. "The Winning Shirt!" shouted Stevie, excitedly. "You didn't forget!"

"How could I forget a promise I made to you?" Dave said, giving his sister a hug.

Stevie grinned, a big, wide grin. Then she and her friends walked to the car, cheering all the way. When they got to where Mrs. Ames had parked, the car was decorated with blue-and-white streamers hanging from the bumpers, the antenna, and the windows. On the back of the car was a big sign that read, THREE CHEERS FOR STEVIE AND FOUR FRIENDS 4-EVER!

"When did you guys do that?" Stevie gasped excitedly.

"That's why we missed some of the first quarter," explained Molly. "This morning Dave met us at Meg's house and helped us get the sign made and all the stuff ready."

"Oh?" said Stevie. "My mother did say he was meeting 'the girls', but I thought she meant the other girls."

119

"Hey!" said Meg, pretending to be a little mad. "Are there any other girls besides the fabulous Friends 4-Ever?"

Stevie and everybody else laughed as they all piled into the decorated Ameses' car. When Mrs. Ames got near Stevie's climbing tree, Stevie called out, "Stop the car!" Scrambling over her friends, Stevie got out. "I'll walk the rest of the way," she said. "I just want to check something."

"I'll go with you," said Molly.

"Me, too," said Meg.

"Me, three," said Laura.

The four friends got out and three of them waited while Stevie climbed up to the spot where her Secret Note Society notes were placed. She had a feeling there might be something there for her, and she was right. In fact, there were three notes but they all said the same thing:

Dear Stevie,

Friends 'til the Ocean Waves,

Love, *Molly*
Love, *Laura*
Love, Meg

When Meg joins the gifted program at school and is overloaded with work, will she give up her work or her friends? Read Friends 4-Ever #7, FRIENDS 4-EVER MINUS 1.

121